Welcome to
the Order !

~~

- Hannah Arelun

THE ORDER OF THE SAND CASTLE

Second Edition, 2023

ISBN 979-8-9886041-0-5

Ingram Spark
1 Ingram Blvd
La Vergne, TN 37086

www.IngramSpark.com

To the Jersey Shore,

where I spent some of the most
magical days of my childhood.

WELCOME TO
THE ORDER

CONTENTS

CHAPTER ONE

THE BEACHERS

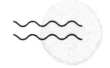

"Wow, seventy-eight degrees, no wind, green flag... what a perfect beach day!" Mr. Beacher exclaims as he sets down a large cooler filled with chips, tumblers of water, sub sandwiches, and even the fresh cubed watermelon that Mrs. Beacher had requested.

"I'm so happy summer is finally here" Mrs. Beacher adds, tipping her face upward to enjoy a kiss from the sun. Already twenty feet ahead of the couple, their daughter, Sands, is running toward, well, seemingly nowhere.

"Race you to the spot!"

Mom, Dad, and older sister, Jane, smile and race the nine-year-old through the soft sand which gives their toes a warm embrace with every step. *Welcome back*, it seems to say. The Beachers have been coming to this beach for years and live on the mainland. Mr. and Mrs. Beacher both work nearby designing environmentally-friendly homes. Jane rules the boardwalk with her gaggle of stylish friends. And Sands, a beach baby from the beginning lives up to her name- always the last out of the water and the last off the beach, sunkissed and sandy from the first day of the summer to the very last minute of it.

"Okay, so who's gonna go body surfing with me today?" says Sands matter-of-factly. Silence. "Come on, you guys are SO boring!"

"I have to tan," says Jane.

"I'm on cooler duty," says Mr. Beacher.

"Come on, Mom," Sands says, pulling on her mom's daisy-yellow sarong.

"How about this? Are you up for some shell collecting? We'll have the first pick of the day," suggests Mrs. Beacher.

"Okay. First shells, then swim," says Sands.

"Wonderful!" says Mrs. Beacher as they get up and head for the promising shoreline.

CHAPTER TWO

TREASURE HUNT

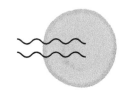

Sands and Mrs. Beacher walk slowly with their eyes glued to the ground, stopping often to crouch down and unearth half-buried treasures. They brush the sand off each new finding, examine it for cracks and interesting colors, and, with the same mannerism, close their eyes briefly to feel for an especially smooth texture.

Mrs. Beacher grew up on the Jersey Shore and, like her daughter, had a curiosity about and love of nature, especially sea creatures. So naturally, she taught Sands everything she knew about the wonderful creatures that share the shoreline, starting with the shells and the kind of things that live inside them.

Beachcomber's Guide to New Jersey Coasts

ATLANTIC SURF CLAM

Spisula solidissima

BLUE MUSSEL

Mytilus edulis

SHARK-EYE SNAIL

Neverita duplicata

MERMAID'S TOENAILS

Anomia simplex

SKATE EGG CASE

Raja eglanteria

DEVIL'S HEAD

Trapa natans

SEA GLASS

Neodymium glass

THREELINE MUDSNAIL

Ilyanassa trivittata

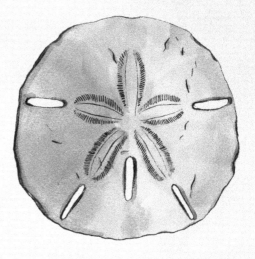

KEYHOLE SAND DOLLAR

Mellita quinquiesperforata

NORTHERN MOONSNAIL

Euspira heros

ATLANTIC SLIPPERSNAIL

Crepidula fornicata

HARDSHELL CLAM

Mercenaria mercenaria

"Mom, why are there so many surf clams but none of the big cool swirly ones...with the pointy part? What are those called again?" asks Sands, lifting a cracked surf clam above her bucket and then dropping it back to the ground.

"Those are whelks, honey. And the pointy parts are called the spires. Do you remember the fun fact I told you about whelks?" Mrs. Beacher replies.

"They're your favorite ones!" Sands proclaims, jumping up out of her crouched position.

Chuckling, Mrs. Beacher says, "Yes, yes, well that too. But also, the knobbed whelk is the official state shell of New Jersey. But I have to say, every year it gets a little harder to find them."

"Aw, that's too bad, they should make more," says Sands.

"Well, that's not up to us, is it? That's the ocean's job. But hey, you know what, I did find an extra cool moon snail." Sands locks eyes longingly on the spherical, pale white shell in her mom's hand.

"Yes...you can have it," says Mrs. Beacher.

Sands gladly accepts and gives her mom a hug with a "Thank you!" before adding it to her bucket. "Now I have two moon snails, five mermaid's toenails, and a million surf clams... but still no sea glass yet. It's impossible to find!"
Sea glass, although not a shell, was Sands' favorite to collect.

"Don't worry, you'll find some. Don't give up!"

~~~~~~

Back at the family spot, a dip in the ocean and a snack later, it was time for Sands' surf lesson. Ready to practice, Sands was quick to say goodbye to her family for the afternoon and join the class.

Walking the short distance to her surf class by way of the waterline, so as to not miss any shells, she spots a brilliantly red crab, cute as can be. She follows it discreetly, getting closer with each step. Then she spots the most curious thing. There looks to be a set of initials written on its back: "OSC." *Could it belong to someone, or it's able to write somehow?* She has to follow it and see where it goes.

Soon, the crab figures out her intentions and picks up its speed. But Sands is quick to follow, bobbing and weaving around people and through holes in the sand. Under the lifeguard stand. Past the jetty... until eventually, they are clear of beach chairs, towels, swimmers, and fishing poles.

Then, seemingly out of nowhere, a lone beach towel appears over a little hill of sand. The crab climbs, and Sands clambers after it. It reaches the edge of the blue-and-white striped towel and ducks underneath.

Aha, got you! Sands thinks as she steps closer and leans to pick up the end of the towel. But as soon as she feels the cloth in her grasp, the ground disappears beneath her. She feels her heart drop, and gravity takes hold of her. She's falling, falling... as the blue sky fades away and then....thud.

What is going on?

CHAPTER THREE

THE ORDER
OF THE
SAND CASTLE

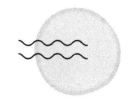

Bewildered and heart racing, Sands wipes the sand out of her eyes and shakes her hair clean. Nothing hurts, so she stands up and tries to assess her arms and legs in the dim light.

She looks up, and the towel seems to have covered the hole again, and she can't see the blue sky above. So where is that dim light coming from? She squints her eyes for the source of the distant glow and can see it getting stronger in one direction. She follows it. *This must be the way out.*

Although a little bit shaken up by her abrupt entry, Sands is not scared. She is in adventure mode. She walks along the cool ground as the light grows brighter.

At the top of a slight hill in the distance, she spots a tall sign. It's made of driftwood like a kid might use for their sand fort, except it's crafted as expertly as if it were a piece of art. It's been carved by a master to show a school of smooth fish circling the inner message: "Property of OSC." *The same letters that are on the back of the crab!* Sands racks her brain for the meaning of the initials. Is it a beach club sign that got washed away? She doesn't know any beach clubs with those initials. The only thing to do is to keep going.

When Sands reaches the top of the hill, the light is now bright enough that she doesn't have to squint anymore. She sees a flag on the horizon that also reads "OSC." As she approaches, the scene below the hill comes into view. Her eyes follow the flagpole down to a tower, then another, then a roof as big as a mansion. No, a castle! A sand castle!

~~~~~

Sands' brain can hardly process what her eyes are taking in at the foot of the immense structure, and any thoughts about making it to her surf lesson vanish. The castle is lit by hundreds of lanterns and surrounded by a massive moat.

As she gets closer, she can see that the exterior is adorned with sea-floor-dwelling creatures of every kind—starfish, sand dollars, snails—and the design is changing in front of her eyes. *They are alive!* And the moat isn't just any old moat. It is filled with fish and other sea creatures. Mesmerized, Sands stares in a trance. Her family is never going to believe this!

Something taps her shoulder, breaking the trance.

"Pretty nice, huh?" a girl's voice says. Sands jumps and turns around. She sees two bright pearls. Eyes? They gleam against a soft pink face, a swirling shell above them. Both enchanting and terrifying, the pearl eyes lock on hers and approach.

"Yes, it's, it's, beautiful..." Sands manages, taking a few steps back.

"How did you find—" the voice demands, but before she can finish, plop! Sands falls backward into the moat. She feels seaweed caress her feet as she swims back up. Pulling her head out of the water, she sees something coming toward her, something she has only seen in movies and once in an aquarium. A fin. Not smooth and rounded like a dolphin's, but sharp and triangular and getting closer by the second. She gasps and closes her eyes for the worst, but nothing happens. She hears the sound of giggling and opens her eyes. The "shark" in front of her isn't really a shark, but seemingly half-boy. His fins flail in amusement and his sharp teeth turn up into a grin as he and the shell-girl gather themselves.

"What is going on!?" a voice calls from above. A flash of feathers descends from a high-up window and lands between the others. "A human...down here. Why did you let her see you?" the winged boy says in a panic.

"Everything is going to be okay!" says Sands in her best impression of her mom. "I didn't mean to upset you. I just followed a crab and somehow it led me here. I'm only here on an adventu—, I mean, by accident."

The girl with the shell on her head puts her hands on her hips and rolls her eyes slightly. "Clawdia!," she calls out. The crab crawls over from afar and puts her claws into the air as if to say *what?* Then everyone loosens up a bit. They have a reason to trust her.

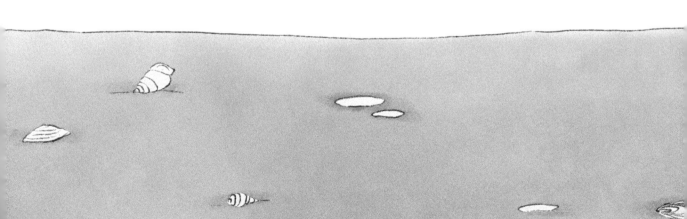

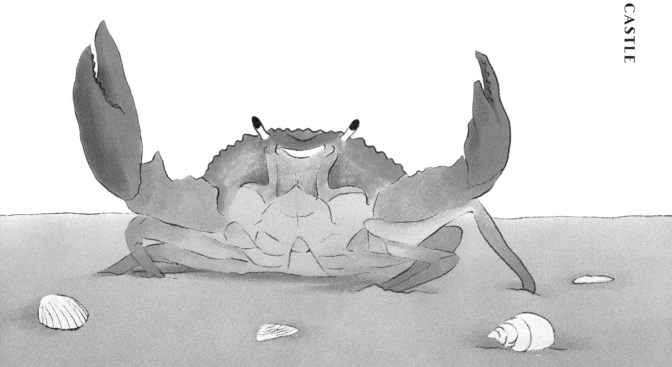

24

CHAPTER FOUR

THE RANGERS

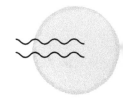

As it turns out, what Sands had thought were monsters are just kids like her... kind of. After the initial shock of their meeting wears off, Sands is introduced to Shelly, Finn, and Piper, three kids that appear to be about her age but with the features of creatures from the sea and sand. They call themselves Rangers for something called The Order of the Sand Castle. The chosen guardians of the beach.

Shelly, the one with the pearl eyes, is strikingly elegant. Her incredibly smooth and gleaming skin is the delicate pink of the inside of a shell. And instead of hair, a large swirling shell sits neatly like a well-hairsprayed up-do. On her shoulder, perched like a broach, sits Clawdia, Shelly's loyal confidant.

Then there is Finn, the hooligan who pranked her, but whose roaring laugh is completely contagious. With deep black eyes, gills on his neck, and the unmissable shark fin on his head, he is intimidating at first, but the sweetest one of the bunch,

Finally, there is Piper. He has long skinny legs, magnificent wings, and a long sharp beak. He moves his head around quickly, checking on things. He is the most mature and responsible of the bunch. Smart, watchful, and protective.

The one thing they have in common, other than being some cross of coastal animal and kid, are their sea glass necklaces, which have an unexplainable glow to them. Each has its own irregular shape and color—Shelly's purple, Finn's blue, and Piper's a frosted amber—and hangs on a string of vibrant seaweed.

Sands, who is wondering why the pieces of sea glass in her collection didn't gleam like that, asks, "What are those necklaces?"

Shelly answers, "For us to do our job protecting the beach, we can't just stay down here, as fabulous as it is! But we can't exactly be walking and swimming around up there in front of all those people, looking like this."

"Yeah," Finn chimes in. "Remember how you reacted to me? Well, it would be even worse if people saw me walking around out of the water."

"And that's where these come in!" Shelly holds her charm tightly in her hand. Slowly, in a mist of purple, she transforms in front of her eyes from a magical creature to a completely human-looking girl. She sports swirling dark braids but still has the brightness of pearls in her eyes.

"Wow, that's magic!" says Sands.

"Not just magic!" pipes in Piper. "Atlantica's magic. She gave us these to help us on our mission of protecting

the beach."

"Atlantica?" asks Sands. The three Rangers' jaws drop.

"She doesn't even know who Atlantica is?" says Finn.

"Is she a big deal?" asks Sands.

Piper continues, "She's kind of the biggest deal. Atlantica is the guardian of the entire eastern seaboard, so everything you can see from here, and further. She's basically a queen. She's in charge of us because she's as old as the ocean itself, and knows everything there is to know about it. We've all sworn an oath to help her protect this beach."

"She literally wrote the book on how to do it," says Shelly. "Piper, show her the book!"

Piper produces a book that was tucked neatly between

his feathers and holds it in front of Sands. The cover reads:

THE COASTAL CODE TO MARINE HARMONY

for use of

THE ORDER OF THE SAND CASTLE

Sands only gets to marvel at it for a second before Piper stows it back in its safe place, ruffling his feathers until the thick book disappears beneath them.

"Wow, she has a lot of rules. More than my mom. So where does Atlantica live? In the castle?" asks Sands.

"Not exactly. She's pretty busy out in the ocean most of the time—guiding whales with her sonar, helping clean and free animals in the great Pacific garbage island, and whatnot. But she did build this castle a long, long time ago. And she comes to visit now and again with the most marvelous stories and news," says Piper.

"And in between, we check in with her on the Worldwide Whelk interjects Shelly.

"I know what a whelk is! My mom loves those," erupts Sands.

"This isn't just any whelk. This one connects us to the entire ocean, and it lets us talk to Atlantica from hundreds of miles away!" Shelly explains. "But on today of all days when we have a new guest to tell her about, it's gone missing. In fact, Clawdia was looking for it when you found her."

Clawdia raises her claws as if to say, *I tried.*

"She probably would want to know about you coming here, too. She's not a big fan of having anyone other than Rangers here. But you do seem fun...courageous for sure!" says Finn.

Sands looks around at her glorious surroundings. She doesn't want to leave. She is already warming up to her new friends. Staring up at the castle and imagining all the fun she could have there, she thinks of an amazing idea.

"You're right, Finn, I am courageous! Maybe you could make me a Ranger so we can hang out some more."

"Hmm, interesting," Finn says. The three Rangers huddle and start whispering. "She's a human," "She's different," "The rules are the rules," and "She can follow them, I'm sure!"

Shelly speaks first. "Okay, if you want to be part of The Order of the Sand Castle, you have to learn to follow all of the rules, and that means helping us take care of the beach."

"And!" Piper jumps in with his pinky finger—or rather, pinky feather—outstretched, "You have to swear to keep us a secret." Sands looks Piper in the eyes and hooks her finger around his smooth feather.

"I promise. I won't let you down."

"Well," says Finn, "then let's call today your first lesson. Why don't you follow us inside and familiarize yourself with the material."

~~~~~

The Rangers lead Sands through the castle's grand entrance and she feels as though she is in a dream. The inside of the castle is just as incredible as the outside—woven seaweed carpets, sculpted archways, mosaic floors of sea stones and broken shells.

As they pass what must be one of the many living rooms, Sands eyes a detailed collage above a sand-carved fireplace; a family portrait of the three Rangers.

"How did you...?" Sands ponders the detailed smiles on their faces.

Shelly answers, "Plastic washes up in every color under the sun, might as well put some use to it!" Curious to explore further, but eager to fulfill her promise, Sands unglues her eyes from the recycled artwork and follows the Rangers.

Reaching a cozy library, she is invited to sit on a driftwood chair around a beautiful round matching table. Piper hands Sands the book and he, Shelly, and Finn all peek over Sands' shoulder to see her reaction as she flips through the pages. Sands' head swirls as she learns about all it takes to protect the beach, and feels a little guilty that she hadn't known these rules before, but more so fulfilled with the sense of purpose she has gained. Watching the seagull-feathered hands of the library's clock, Sands waits until the last minute that she can sneak back to her family unnoticed. But before she leaves, she arranges to meet her new friends the very next day to resume her learning. *This is going to be the best summer ever,* she thinks as she waves goodbye.

CHAPTER FIVE

BY THE BOOK

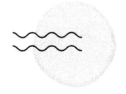

After their initial meeting, the new friends become quickly inseparable. Sands meets with the Rangers every day, book in hand, to survey the beach and learn how to follow the rules.

On Tuesday, they run into a group of seagulls feasting on a bag of chips.

"Rule #22, don't feed the birds," says Piper as he collects the bag despite the seagulls' look of protest. "They may want to eat human food, but it's actually bad for their diet and can make them sick. Plus, if they become dependent on human food, they lose touch with the hunting instincts that they need to survive."

On Wednesday, they spot a struggling horseshoe crab stuck on its back, and the rangers teach Sands the right way to gently turn it over from the side of its shell.

"Rule #45," says Shelly, "never leave a horseshoe crab stuck on its back. When that happens, they need our help. And Rule #46: Never pick up a horseshoe crab by its tail, only its shell...You see, their tails are extremely delicate. If it is injured or detached, the horseshoe crab won't be able to navigate the water."

"Yeah," Finn adds, "and these guys have been around longer than any of us, I'm talking millions of years. They aren't technically even crabs, which is also why they are completely harmless, they don't have sharp claws to pinch with. I love those little Arthropods!"

On Thursday, they repair the fences around the dunes. "These dunes look like they might be a fun place to play around, but they are crucial to the sea birds that nest in them," says Piper. He puts two fingers in between his lips and whistles a perfect bird call. A few seconds later, a near-distant whistle replies. "Wanna see?"

Piper walks along the fence. Then he stops and leans far over the top. He lifts a few strands of drooping seagrass to reveal the reply whistle's owner—a small sandpiper bird sitting gently on a nest of even smaller eggs, white with brown speckles. Piper whistles again, this time in something that sounds like a full sentence. His feathered friend flaps her wings and nods

in response. "Seaerra says thank you for fixing the fence and protecting her little ones."

On Friday, they put on gloves and scour the beach for trash, collecting plastic bags of every shape and color. "This is one of the biggest jobs, which is why we do it every week."

~~~

Later that day, after lugging bags of trash and recycling to the bins to be collected, the team celebrates a job well done back at the castle, doing cannonballs into the moat and eating ice cream cones. They offer Sands strange flavors—seaweed, shrimp, and red algae—but thankfully they have some sea salt chocolate which Sands politely selects.

"We've never met a kid like you before," says Finn.

"You've respected our rules, the beach, and its creatures. Especially us. That's why we have a really special surprise for you. Shelly, would you do the honors?"

"Sands Beacher of beyond the dunes, we'd like to officially unofficially invite you to be part of The Order of the Sand Castle." Shelly reveals a necklace with a green sea glass charm and gently places it over Sands' head.

Piper adds, "It might not be magic like ours, but it is really special. It's a symbol of our friendship and loyalty and–" Clawdia crawls over and snips at Piper's ankle. "And Clawdia spent all day looking for just the right one for you." Sands hugs each of her friends and picks up Clawdia.

"It's absolutely perfect."

#2. TREAT THE BEACH LIKE A FRIEND

#3. CARE FOR THE BEACH'S MANY CREATURES

#4. RESPECT THE NATURAL HABITAT

#5. ALWAYS BE KIND TO YOUR FELLOW RANGER

#6. WORK TOGETHER; RANGERS ARE STRONGER TOGETHER

#7. NEVER TAKE A LIVING THING OUT OF ITS HOME

ONE OF THE GANG

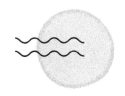

Everything is going more wonderfully with her new friends than Sands could have ever imagined. Now that they can roam the beach freely, Sands has introduced the Rangers to her family, explaining that they are new kids who have just moved into their area.

Her parents find the group's serious demeanor adorable, thinking their chatter about missions, sea queens, and castles is part of a game of make-believe. They are happy to see Sands' energy matched and the exhausted look of satisfaction she always has on the walk home.

Things feel comfortable, and Sands now knows the rule book like the back of her hand. Now, they regularly quiz her as they walk around between missions.

Today, Piper rattles off a series of quizzes by number. "Rule #7?"

"Easy, never take a living thing out of its home," says Sands.

"Okay, big shot, Rule #30?"

"I remember from that party last week. Never let go of a balloon at the beach."

"Okay, good one, what about rule #17?"

"#17: Always pick up your dog's...#2!"

"Gross but important. Wow, you are really getting the hang of this!"

"Thanks, Piper," says Sands. "I do have the most fabulous teachers! But anyway, since we've been working so hard at lessons, I have an idea."

"What is it?" Finn asks excitedly. "More ice cream? A nice long swim?"

"Not quite, but I think you're gonna love it, Finn. Since you guys have shown me how to do so many things, I thought I might show you what I know about the beach."

"Like human stuff?" Shelly asks.

"Not just human stuff—kid human stuff. I'm gonna show you how to play!" The Rangers think for a second. They have seen humans playing and doing all kinds of activities from afar, but they never thought to get involved. But with all the help from Sands, they are ahead on their duties, and they still haven't gotten any new assignments or news from Atlantica, with the Worldwide Whelk still being lost.

"I mean, learning more about humans might be good for our mission," says Shelly.

"Yeah, it would be more research than anything," adds Piper.

"Who cares about research!? You heard Sands, let's have some fun! Where do we start?" bursts out Finn.

"Well, you know that surf class I go to, there's always room for a few more!"

CHAPTER SEVEN

FUN IN THE SUN

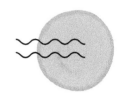

With no fear of the water and its waves, the Rangers are quick to tackle surfing. They jump into the water with more confidence than the teachers have ever seen in beginners.

Even in his disguised state, Piper paddles with the speed and stamina of his wings. Finn's natural connection to the surfboard's bottom fin helps him catch waves at just the right moment. But it's Shelly's steady and smooth movement that helps her catch a first wave before any of them, seemingly sticking to the board like a snail.

"Swimming is great, and flying can't be beaten, but this is like flying on the water," says Piper.

"I've always wanted to know what it feels like to fly!" says Finn, flapping his arms.

"Guys, I need, need, NEED a surfboard!" Shelly yells as she excitedly shakes the board under her.

"Everybody, as you may have noticed, we have a few new students today, and it looks like they are naturals!" the surf teacher, Matt, announces. "So make sure you welcome Shelly, Finn, and Piper out there."

The children answer in chorus, "Welcome," and the Rangers wave back shyly. They are confident in the waves, but they are just getting used to meeting so many humans. But as the afternoon goes on, the kids are quick to get to know the Rangers, complimenting their moves and their cool necklaces, and asking lots of questions.

"Where do you live?"

"Pretty close, actually. Just south of here."

"Where do you go to school?"

"Umm, it's a very small specialized school, focusing on marine biology."

"Are you siblings?"

"Puh-lease, we're not even the same species!"

With each passing wave, the Rangers grow less wary and more fond of the other kids. Humans could be so nice. They couldn't wait to tell Atlantica about all they had seen, heard, and experienced.

CHAPTER EIGHT

WHAT THE TIDE BROUGHT IN

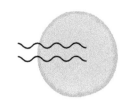

After weeks of amazing weather, a raging storm arrives. At the Beacher's home up the road from the beach, trees shake, rain whips at the windows, and the power goes out. Sands imagines huge waves crashing onto the beach and hopes her friends are safe beneath them. More than that, she misses them. It's the first day she hasn't been to the beach all summer. She passes the time by counting and recounting her shell collection and waxing her already-waxed surfboard.

Two days later, sunshine prevails. Birds chirp in celebration. It is without a doubt, "Time to go to the beach!" Sands screams, bouncing onto the foot of her parents' bed, bathing suit and sunscreen already on.

"Okay, darling, why don't you go pack some towels while

we get up—"

"Done!" She interrupts her mom mid-sentence.

After Sands chokes down a bowl of cereal and paces up and down the hallway for a bit, the Beachers are finally on their way to their favorite place.

~~~~

Of course, when they get to the beach, Sands can hardly sit still. She turns down her mom's offer to go shell searching and even lets her dad take the first dip into the ocean solo. She has places to be and people to see. *To the sand castle!*

Sands sets out quickly to the secret entrance. Seeing the towel in its place, waiting for her arrival like always, she knows everything is all right. She jumps onto it, sending herself down the familiar chute. "Cannonball!" she yells in excitement. She sticks the landing and calls out to her friends, "Shelly, Finn, Piper! I'm back, I'm back!"

United again, the group laughs and hugs and then updates Sands about the storm. "You see, the castle is protected by Atlantica's magic, so it's totally invincible in any storm. But during storms, lots of things can get washed ashore, so today is going to be a very busy day."

The group heads out, following the shore to collect washed-up trash, rescue fish from shrinking tide pools, and right toppled-over horseshoe crabs. It is, as predicted, a busy day.

Eventually, Sands senses it's time for a break and leads

the group back to her family's spot for a snack. As they sink their teeth into watermelon cubes and crunch away at salty pretzels, Mrs. Beacher approaches them excitedly.

"Kids, you'll never believe what I found by the water. It must have washed up in the storm." She reaches into the bucket and pulls out a massive, perfectly formed shell. "Have you ever seen a knobbed whelk so big? Isn't it amazing?"

"The Worldwide Whelk!" Piper exclaims. "Excuse me, Mrs. Beacher, can you check if there is anything written in that shell? We had an identical one that just went missing."

"Hmm, let's see....gosh you're right! It says OSC. What's that?" Before Piper answers out of excitement, Sands butts in.

"It's for our play-pretend club!"

"Well, play on kids," she says, handing the shell over to their eager little hands. "What amazing luck. Almost like magic that it found its way back to you."

"Yeah, almost!" Shelly says, winking at Sands.

~~~

Walking her friends back to the sand castle, Sands is impatient to get out of earshot of her family to see how this magical shell device works. "What do you? Like, just hold it up to your ear like a phone or something?" she asks Shelly.

"If it was that obvious, people would be onto us right away. No, these have gotten a lot better since the old days when we used flip-shell phones." Shelly uses her fingers to trace the Worldwide Whelk's swirl in a memorized combination of movements and then presses the pointed top. "And there," she says.

From within the hole of the shell, a screen projects with the quality of sunshine. She types something on the holographic screen, setting off the looping sound of a whale's call. "It's ringing," Shelly declares, but no one answers. "Atlantica must be busy still. We'll leave her a message, and I'm sure she'll be back in no time. Then she'll come and you can meet her and it will be awesome!"

CHAPTER NINE

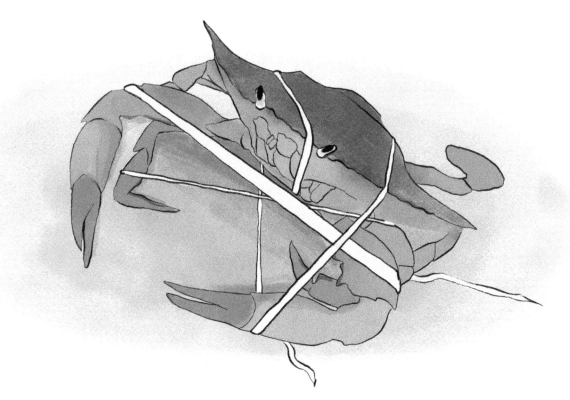

LETTING GO

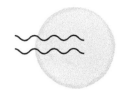

The next day is another busy one, but Sands is still thinking about the Worldwide Whelk and its unanswered call. She wants to do a great job so that she can impress Atlantica when she answers.

Out on the crew's daily mission, they check the dune fences, look for litter around the jetties, and even free a crab from a tangled balloon string. Clawdia uses her nimble claws to cut through the knots and embraces her freed friend.

Piper stews with anger over the sight of yet another tangled mess. "I can't believe people just keep leaving these things behind. They are terrible. They go up, and people act like they are disappearing into the sky. But every time, they come back down and become a hazard for the beach. They just can't learn, can they?"

"I think you're right," Sands says.

"Thank you! It's like people don't even know."

"But, Piper, that's just it!"

"What's just it?"

"You know, people, kids, they just don't know about the beach like you do, and they really can't learn without some help. It's just like the people who feed the birds. They just think they must be starving! Or think the dune is just a fun little hill. I think we should start giving people beach lessons. You know, like you did for me."

"But, Sands," Finn says, "Not everyone is like you. And besides, we are supposed to help the beach. Talking to people about it has never been part of our directions."

"Guys, listen! Instead of spending so much time picking up and repairing and whatnot, we could stop it from happening. Look, you met me and my family and even all those nice kids at surf camp. We're not all perfect, but we can do better. We just need to learn." The group weighs this in their minds. "Besides, what do we have to lose?" Sands asks.

Piper scratches his head. Shelly recedes a little into herself. Finn looks into the sky in thought. And then, breaking the silence, Clawdia lifts her claws into the air as if to say *why not?* Impressed and inspired by the bravery of their smallest comrade, the others nod.

"Let's do it," says Piper. "For the beach."

~~~~~

After that decision, the Order's days and routines begin to change. With a new angle to their mission, and their leader still out of contact, the kids figure out their new way to protect the beach. At first, the crew is shy, just like in surf class. But soon, as people begin to thank them for their advice and promise to do better, they walk a little taller and looser as they approach the numerous beach circles, sunbathers, and swimmers across the beach.

"Did you know that plastic can end up in the ocean, even if you don't litter? Bringing reusable water bottles to and from the beach works great. And it usually keeps your water colder for longer!"

"Excuse me, and happy birthday. I hope you are having a great party. But if you don't mind, please don't let those balloons go while you're outdoors. In fact, balloons should be avoided altogether, or kept inside to avoid any accidental releases. Animals may not only get tangled in them, but they may mistake the balloon for food and eat it which can make them sick."

"Hi there, and hello to you, cutie! We love seeing your dog at the beach, but we noticed he sometimes buries his, umm, you know what. If you use a bag to scoop it up and throw it in the trash, it would help the beach a lot."

As the days go by, the success of their new strategy becomes unquestionable. There is less litter, and more thoughtful decisions being made. And despite the fact that the Rangers have been trying to lie low, they are becoming friends with all the beachgoers. People wave at them on their rounds. They ask questions about wildlife. And some of the regular shell searchers even join them to pick up litter instead.

Near the end of another great day of progress, the crew takes a break to play frisbee and revel in their excitement.

Shelly throws to Piper and says, "Wow, we're cutting our work in half and having twice as much fun!"

"I know, and the beach is looking so beautiful," he replies, "And I think people are having a good time learning too." Piper throws to Finn.

"Speaking of learning," Finn replies, "I can't wait to tell Atlantica all about this. She's going to be so impressed with how we've been doing." Overly energized by his excitement, Finn rips a strong throw in the direction of Sands, but the frisbee lands in the ocean. She laughs, happy to see her friends so full of joy.

"I'll get it!" Sands runs to the water and splashes through the gentle current, then plunges after the frisbee.

CHAPTER TEN

ATLANTICA

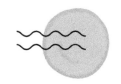

Searching where she thought she had seen the toy go, Sands finally sees a glimmer of color beneath the waves. She reaches down, expecting to feel the smooth side of the frisbee, but the texture she comes in contact with is a bit bumpier and slimier.

As she picks up the mysterious object, glowing light breaks through the surface, revealing a cast of vibrant colors—purple, orange, pink. Looking down at her hands, Sands sees the most beautiful starfish she has ever encountered. Its wiggling legs are full of life, and she giggles at the ticklish sensation and sheer brilliance.

Sands looks back to the beach where Shelly, Finn, and Piper are awaiting her return, then back at the incredible creature in her palm. She thinks, "Rule #6, never take a living thing out of its home." But on the other hand, *my friends need to see this*. If I leave it now, I may never find it again.

After a few more seconds of deliberation, Sands shifts her body back toward the shore. "It will just be a minute, then I'll put you right back where you belong," she whispers to the star while stroking its glittering arms. But not one step into her return, the water starts swirling angrily around her. The sand locks her feet in place, and then something—something big, something fish-like—emerges from the water.

"I am Atlantica, guardian of the eastern seaboard." Two large dark eyes stare back at her. A crown of barnacle sits on her head, circling a blow-hole from which shimmering locks of water spout. "You, human, have failed my test."

Sands looks up wide-eyed. "I was going to put it back, I swear!"

Atlantica counters, "Your friends were wrong about you. You're exactly why we exist, why we have to protect these beaches! The real failure here belongs to Shelly, Finn, and Piper. I let them out of my sight for one day, and they forget the #1 rule of The Order of the Sand Castle: Don't trust humans."

Sands stops fighting the sand gripping her ankles and sinks a little deeper. *The one rule they wouldn't tell me.* It dawned on her, *They risked everything for me. And I ruined it.*

Atlantica wasn't yet done. "As punishment, I will remind them what the humans cost us." She wields a driftwood staff, raising it high into the air and then bringing it down with fury. A booming sound reverberates through the air, but the beach remains calm to the naked eye.

"What did you do?" yelps Sands.

"I've brought the sand castle down so those three children can see what it's like to have to build it from the ground up, like I had to do when we were first overrun by chairs, bonfires, and bulldozers, long ago," Atlantica finishes, her pure anger giving way to signs of a deep sadness. With one swift strike of her fins, she snatches Sands' sea glass necklace from around her neck. "As for you, small human, stay away from my Rangers and try not to cause any more damage than you already have."

With another sway of her staff, Atlantica manipulates the current to pull Sands far away from her friends and back towards the beachgoers. She reaches towards Pearl, Finn, and Piper, but they are now focused on Atlantica, who is delivering the bad news.

Thrust by one final wave, Sands thumps back onto the beach, still clutching the cursed starfish. She looks at it with confused, tear-filled eyes, and as she wipes them with her hand, the starfish vanishes, a mere illusion as part of her test. Gone as fast as her new world and friends.

She trudges back to her towel, trying to gather her emotions, and rejoins her family, making up a story about a body-surfing wipeout to explain the tears. "Can we go home now?"

CHAPTER ELEVEN

THE SAND PILE

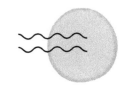

The next day Sands doesn't spring out of bed like usual. After a night of tossing and turning, and replaying the events in her head, she closes her blinds to the sunny day and pulls her covers over her face.

She pictures her friends' likely restless night in the ruins of their castle. Shelly squeezing into her shell, trying not to look at or think about the mess. Piper feeling exposed without his usual patch of seagrass to rest in. And Finn pacing around instead of dreamily gliding through the moat. (Like most sharks, he didn't sleep but loved to let his mind rest while taking slow laps in the water.)

When Mrs. Beacher comes in to check on her, Sands pretends to be sick, coughing unconvincingly into her elbow.

"Well, your temperature is fine, and it's the middle of August," says Mrs. Beacher. "I can't think of any other reason you wouldn't want to go to the beach on a beautiful day. I'm sure your friends will miss you!"

"I doubt it," says Sands. "I'm a bad friend."

"Well, I've been your friend for a long, long time now, and I don't think that's true. What happened?"

Without thinking about it, Sands blurts out. "I didn't follow the rules, and I ruined their amazing sand castle, and now I ruined everything!" She falls into her mom's open arms.

"Oh, Sands, it will be all right. It's just a sand castle. Why don't you help them rebuild it?"

"I wish I could but it's huge, even the four of us could

never do it." Mrs. Beacher wasn't used to her ambitious daughter turning down a challenge.

"Hmm, well, you've seen your dad and I design houses around town, and I've built quite a few sand castles in my day. Why don't you let us help?" says Mrs. Beacher.

"Thanks, Mom, but I don't know, " says Sands.

"And your sister, she thinks your friends are great, I'm sure she'd help," continues Mrs. Beacher. Sands could see the hope in her mom's eyes and wanted it to be that easy. But if even her sister wanted to help... The Rangers had made so many friends at the beach the last couple of weeks. Maybe, just maybe...

"Okay, I'll be ready in ten!"

~~~~~

After reiterating to her family the importance of the sand castle over and over on the way over, and explaining its size, Sands hits the beach with renewed hope and a mission. She goes from towel to towel, explaining that the Rangers need all the help they can get. It is an emergency. And one by one, everyone from the woman with the dog to the birthday party guests to the tanners, fishers, and surfers, gathers with Sands, eager to help.

"Okay, guys, follow me!"

As directed, the beachgoers follow Sands to where she has always found the beach towel lying, but when she gets closer and doesn't see the blue stripes anywhere, she begins to panic. "It's gotta be here, it's gotta be! Finn, Shelly, Piper! Please let me apologize, please let me help!" she yells into the breeze.

The group grows weary. Was this girl just stuck in a game of pretend, and just dragging them along?

"Please, let me in!" Sands goes down to her hands and knees and tries to dig her way to the entrance. Then, just as she can feel the tears welling up like the tide, she sees a flash of red. "Clawdia!" The small crab gestures for Sands to follow her until she reaches a small twig in the sand and points. *It's right here.*

A few strides behind her, the crowd of people watch as Sands steps over the twig and miraculously vanishes into the sand. Flabbergasted, they stare at the space where she once stood, just to see the small crab wave them forward.

"I'm going after her," says Mrs. Beacher. Then one by one, the crew follows into the unknown.

~~~~

Now underground, and humbled by disbelief, the group quietly follows Sands and Clawdia past the "Property of OSC" sign and down to a mountain of sand riddled with stray shells and half-buried driftwood furniture.

"Wow, I thought it was just a game," says Mr. Beacher. Then the group sees Shelly, Finn, and Piper. But it's not the Shelly, Finn, and Piper they are used to. The Rangers are in their natural form—feathers, fins, and all.

Both the humans and the Rangers gasp in surprise. The Rangers reach for their necklaces and begin to shift form.

"No!" protests Mrs. Beacher. "We're in your space. Be comfortable just as you are. We are your friends, and you are incredible." The Rangers feel a warm rush of acceptance, quelling their fear instantly.

"Yeah!" says one of the kids from the surf class. "No wonder you were such great surfers."

Then a sun-tanning regular chimes in, "You have made the beach so much better—cleaner and happier! The least we can do is help you rebuild your home."

"Yup, that's the plan!" says Sands. Everyone stares at the mountain of ruin. And then they go to work.

Piper digs into the library to fish out an old scroll laying out the drawings for the sand castle—measurements, labels for rooms, and even furniture designs.

"These plans will do great!" says Mr. Beacher.

Then everyone splits up into groups and gets down to work. Mr. and Mrs. Beacher help use their architectural skills to translate the floor plans. The kids gather shovels to start digging things out, while Finn digs with powerful swipes of his tail. The lifeguard directs groups of helpers with his whistle. Shelly burrows under the sand to retrieve furniture and tools and valuables, while Piper flits about, gathering things from the top of the sand mountain.

At the end of the day, everyone's arms grow tired, and then more tired. They put down their shovels and tools for the night, promising to resume their work the next day.

CHAPTER TWELVE

RESURFACING

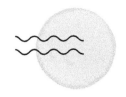

Not long after the sun begins to peek over the ocean's horizon, the Rangers' new crew of helpers plop into the underground fortress. This time, they bring ladders, coolers of food and drink, and a stereo. The humans—once strangers but now friends—push up their sleeves and get back to work rebuilding the beautiful structure. And everyone is having fun doing it.

Piper flies around swiftly in circles, delivering tools to people on ladders, while Shelly teaches kids to direct sand dollars and crustaceans and other small creatures back to the walls to sparkle as beautiful guests. Finn swims around the newly built moat, handing out snacks and giving people rides to different parts of the work site.

Sands' heart warms as she arrives and sees her two worlds come together. She approaches Shelly as she orchestrates a family of starfish to sit symmetrically between two large windows.

"Sands, finally! Doesn't it look beautiful?" says Shelly, her pearly eyes looking brighter than ever.

"It does," says Sands. "Sorry for being late. I wanted to bring something for you. Something that belongs to you. Well, they belonged to the beach all along." Sands gestures to an overflowing pail of assorted shells in her hands; her prized collection.

"The perfect finishing touch," says Shelly. "Don't worry, Sands, you can come and enjoy them anytime. I know hermit crabs who are going to love these." Shelly walks over the edge of the moat, drops the shells on the ground, and whistles. Slowly, small crabs crawl their way to the piles. Some take their shells off and try on new ones, which they proudly display, modeling to each other. Sands and Shelly giggle. Hermit crabs are such fashionistas. As a thank-you, the hermit crabs scuttle onto the wall, forming a heart.

The people and the Rangers leave their workstations, and fold up their ladders to admire their incredible feat. Sitting at the foot of the awesome structure, sweaty, exhausted, and sand covered, their hearts hum with pride and happiness. But wait... there was an actual humming, or more of a rumbling. The ground begins to quiver. *Are we falling?* Sands thinks in a panic. *What have we done wrong?* Above, the ceiling parts, sending a flurry of sand through the air, and morning sunlight streams over their faces. They aren't falling at all— they're being lifted. The whole castle is being raised to the surface.

"What in the name of Poseidon...?" Piper mutters as the sand castle and all of its rebuilders settle at beach level, facing the glittering ocean.

"Forget Poseidon," says Finn, "it's Atlantica!" Fins and staff raised in the air, Atlantica hovers out of the water, radiating sheer greatness. To the Rangers' surprise, she wears a brimming smile that seems to span the entire horizon. Everyone in the audience is speechless when she speaks.

"My Rangers," she calls out, "and my new friends, our new human friends. I owe you a great apology, and I've come to set things right. You've shown me that humans and the sea can live together in harmony once again. No more hiding and secrets. This sand castle, this symbol of friendship, will now stand in the light for all to enjoy. Protected by my magic, it shall be a center dedicated to education and conservation, and of course, friendship."

Sands is the first to react. Wading into the ocean, she approaches the magnificent guardian she once feared and embraces her in a hug. "Oh, thank you, thank you Atlantica."

Atlantica pulls Sands' sea glass necklace out of her loyal barnacles. "I believe this is yours, Ranger Sands," she says.

"Thank you. And welcome, forever, to The Order of the Sand Castle." She places the necklace over Sands' head and with one more wave to the beach, disappears back into the deep.

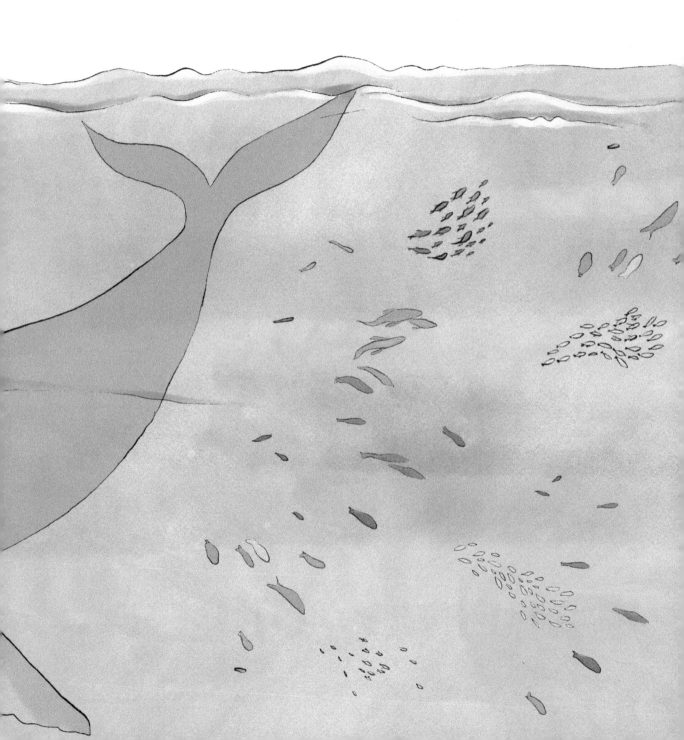

CHAPTER THIRTEEN

THE NEW ORDER

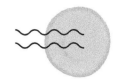

After Atlantica's visit, The Order of the Sand Castle evolves from a secretive organization to a welcome center to teach humans about the beach and how to help it thrive. By the time the summer nears its end, so much has changed. The halls of the sand castle are now more alive than ever. Its classrooms are full of children, and there are celebrations of pure joy. Shelly, Finn, and Piper no longer use their human forms but are well-loved for their unique features and abilities. The beach is cleaner, and its animals feel safe and at home.

Today, the last day of summer, the afternoon sun kisses the sky with gold and peach, a dramatic end to one unforgettable season. Now, there is only one thing left to do.

"Surf's up!" yells Finn, racing his friends into the waves.

AUTHOR'S NOTE

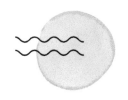

Hannah Anderson is a copywriter and author who grew up in Fair Haven, New Jersey and attended Northwestern University. Devoted to a life with her feet in the sand and her head in the clouds, Hannah's adventurous spirit and vivid imagination fuel her diverse creative endeavors.

An animal and nature lover at heart, Hannah is passionate about conservation, especially when it comes to her beloved Jersey Shore. From playing in the sand to riding waves to running the boardwalk, the inspiration and love that she has put into her writing have been years in the making.

Hannah wrote The Order of The Sand Castle to remind children and their families of the magic of our environment, and our responsibility to protect it. For summers to come, she hopes to inspire readers from Sandy Hook to Cape May and beyond with her whimsical narrative, lovable characters, and timeless message.

THANK YOU

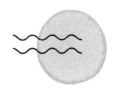

To my friends and family who supported my passion project from the start. Especially my mom, dad, and grandmother who were the first to read it.

To my incredible illustrator and partner, Nimisha; this book wouldn't have been possible without you.

To Clean Ocean Action for supporting the local environment that inspired this book.

And to all those who follow the mission of The Order of the Sand Castle, taking action to protect and preserve our magnificent shores.

Printed in the USA
CPSIA information can be obtained
at www.ICGtesting.com
LVHW071826101023
760619LV00001B/1

9 798988 604106